Crush

by Jon Blake

Illustrated by Peter Richardson

Introduction

Jamal's got a crush on Rachelle. When Ian finds out, he makes Jamal's life hell. But Ian's got his own secret love. He's written her name all through his exercise book. When the book goes missing, it's time to stage a desperate cover-up.

Who's who

On the outside, Ian's just one of the lads. But there's a more sensitive side to Ian. He just makes sure no one knows about it.

Leanne likes attention. She's cool, and when she needs to be, she's cruel. But that's just her sense of humour.

Jamal's basically a decent person. But he's easily wound up, and the class wind him up as often as possible. That's probably why he throws such wobblies.

Chapter 1

My name is Ian Street. Something painful happened to me the other week. It all began when Mrs Walker (our form teacher) brought a video camera into class.

"Does anyone know what this is?" she asked.

Ten voices answered at once:

"JVC, Miss!"

"My dad's got one of them, Miss!"

"Are we going to make a horror movie, Miss?"

Mrs Walker called for silence.

"This is a video camera," she said, "and if you are *sensible,* we are going to use it in Media Studies."

Mrs Walker's plan was simple. She would explain how the camera worked, then everyone would make a one-minute video.

Some hope.

Michelle went first. She thought the camera was off when it was on, and made a lovely film of her feet.

Bashir's film flew about all over the place. It went from the ceiling to the light switch to Mrs Walker, telling him to give the camera back.

Third was Marlowe. He made a classic called "Darkness", which was all black, seeing as he forgot to take the lens cap off.

That was enough for Mrs Walker. She decided to organize the next video properly. We set up some chairs, a table and a cactus. Leanne was the interviewer, and Jamal was the guest. I was on camera.

I focused the camera on Leanne. She had obviously been waiting for this day all her life. Leanne was Miss Supercool, with her hands neatly crossed and her eyes rock steady. Jamal, on the other hand, was Coco the Clown.

"Action," I cried.

Leanne began to speak, very clearly and politely, in a voice like Princess Di. She asked Jamal where he was born, if he had a large family, what he thought of his teachers, and what his best sport was. She nodded calmly at his answers. All the while she was smiling a little smile. Then, out of the blue, she threw in a new question.

"Jamal, do you have much in common?"

Jamal was puzzled.

"Who with?" he asked.

"With Rachelle Parris," replied Leanne.

Jamal's face dropped. "Shut up!" he snapped.

Everyone laughed. We all knew Jamal had a thing about Rachelle.

"Do you like Rachelle Parris?" asked Leanne.

"No," snapped Jamal.

"I hope you're telling the truth, Jamal," said Leanne, sternly.

At this point Jamal made things ten times worse for himself.

He said he didn't like any girls, that they were all stupid, boring, ugly and useless at cricket. By the time he had finished, it was completely obvious he was in love.

Leanne smiled sweetly and shook Jamal by the hand. "Thank you, Jamal," she said.

With that, Leanne jumped up, sang the theme song from *Surprise, Surprise* and did a few dance steps. By now the class was in stitches and I couldn't keep the camera steady at all.

Mrs Walker had missed everything. She'd been out of the room talking to the Head. When she came back we asked if we could show the video to the rest of the school.

"No!" said Jamal.

"Why, what's the matter, Jamal?" asked Mrs Walker.

Jamal was silent. Mrs Walker suspected something. "I think we'll wait till we can make a really top-class video." she said.

We decided to show it anyway.

Chapter 2

Poor old Jamal. It just wasn't his day. By the end of the dinner hour, at least a hundred people had seen our video. Some of them had seen it twice, and all of them wanted more.

We agreed to make another chat show in a week's time, but oddly enough, Jamal wasn't keen.

That afternoon our classroom was like Waterloo Station. People were rushing in with all kinds of messages for Jamal. Some said Rachelle wanted to see him at once. Others said Rachelle had been seen with another boy. One said Rachelle was crying because Jamal was ignoring her.

It wasn't true that Rachelle was crying, but it was certainly true that Jamal was ignoring her. Normally he was buzzing round her all the time. Now he couldn't even remember who she was.

The trouble with Jamal was that he was easy to wind up. I couldn't resist it. I sent him a message across class:

Jamal darling, lets name the day on the chat show next week.
Rachelle

Jamal didn't find it very funny. He shook his fist at me.

That evening I told the family what had happened. I described my expert camerawork, and how Leanne took Jamal apart, and what was happening on the next show. My big sister Jo wasn't impressed.

"You wouldn't like it if it happened to you," she said.

"It *didn't* happen to me," I said.

I was still thinking back on it when I went to bed. I'd known Leanne since I was five, but I'd never seen her act like that before. Once that camera was on, she was a different person. Very adult, cool and polite. I liked that. I liked it a lot. In fact ...

In *fact* ...

Oh no!

I'd got a crush on her.

Chapter 3

Next morning, there was just one thought in my mind. *No one must know.* No one must see me talking to Leanne, looking at her, or muttering her name under my breath. If anyone got the slightest idea I fancied Leanne, I was finished. I would either have to get plastic surgery or leave the country.

As usual, Leanne was in the playground when I arrived at school.

I'd seen her there a thousand times and hardly noticed her. Today, however, a terrible sick feeling came over me. I wanted everyone else to disappear so it would be just me and her.

Oh no! I was watching her already!

I rushed past her to the school door. Just as I feared, she spoke.

The morning was murder. I had such an urge to look at her in class. In the end I built a little wall of books so I couldn't see her even if I wanted to. Even then I could hear her joking about with Danny and Bash. It made me sick.

Then, that afternoon, the subject of the chat show came up. Everyone agreed that I would be the director, but there was an argument about who would be on the show. Jade wanted to do a version of *Blind Date*, with Rachelle and guess who. Leanne protested. She said she was the best interviewer and should do it again.

Next second, to my horror, a hand landed on my shoulder. Leanne's hand. I came out of my seat like a space rocket.

"I'm trying to work!" I snapped, and marched off.

I went home with my shoulder burning. By the time I got home, the little crush had grown into a massive obsession. I wished I was a girl, because girls were allowed to feel like this. They even enjoyed it.

That evening, I took out an exercise book,
and wrote her name on it: Leanne Grant.
That name had magical powers.

I wrote it again, and again, and again.
I filled a page, then another page, and didn't
stop till I'd finished the book.

I felt a little better now. But I had a new problem. Where would I hide the book? I didn't have anything with a lock on it, and my brothers and sisters were always going through my things. The only answer was to sleep with it, then put it in my school bag next day.

I couldn't get anything right next day. I couldn't even find my shorts for games. I went all through my bag for them, then remembered they were in my locker. I often leave them there for a few weeks, to give them a good blue-cheesy smell. It puts people off tackling me at football.

To get to the lockers I had to go past the South Playground. That was where the girls played netball. There was no way I could get across that playground without one little peek at Leanne.

I crept up alongside the woodwork block, then glanced round the corner. To my surprise, someone was already there, watching the girls.

That someone was Jamal.

Jamal whirled round. He looked guilty.
Next second I was racing towards the footy
pitch, yelling, "Jamal's been watching
Rachelle! Jamal's been watching Rachelle!"

Crunch! I was on the ground. Jamal was hammering me like a punch bag.

"Help!" I cried.

It took four lads to pull him off.

Mrs Walker stopped the games lesson and had us all lined up in shame.

Mrs Walker read us the riot act. "You boys know nothing," she said. "You think you're all so big, but you're not. You're childish and immature. It's time you grew up."

No one liked being told that, especially with the girls listening. "I'll get you for that," said Jamal, when the others had gone. I just laughed. I really hated Jamal now. I sloped off home in a sulk, and emptied my bag all over my bed.

It was then that I noticed that something was missing. The exercise book! In all the commotion, I must have left it in the changing-rooms.

Chapter 4

I was up at seven next morning. I had to get that book before someone else did.

It was a weird feeling being first into school. Not a soul in the playground. No cars in the parking spaces. Just the sound of my own footsteps, running towards the changing-rooms. Just the smell of my own fear as I discovered the exercise book was *not there*.

I couldn't follow a word in assembly. Mr Roberts might as well have been talking Japanese. Could I have dropped the book in the toilets? Could the cleaners have thrown it away? Could aliens have teleported it to a planet humans will never visit?

Someone nudged me. Mr Roberts wanted our attention. "I have here," he said, "an item of lost property." Mr Roberts lifted his hand. In it was an exercise book. "Does anyone recognize this?" he asked. I lowered my head between my knees. That's what you do when you think you're going to faint.

41

"No name on the cover ..." said Mr Roberts.

Thank God for that, I thought.

"Oh ..." said Mr Roberts, "... Leanne Grant."

I couldn't look. I heard Leanne's footsteps going to the front, then her voice: "It's not mine, Mr Roberts."

"But it's got your name all over it," said Mr Roberts.

Please, Death, come quickly, I thought. Anything but this.

"Well, you'd better hang on to it," said Mr Roberts. "I'm sure you must know whose it is."

Assembly ended. The classes filed out, leaving Leanne surrounded by a squeaking gang.

"Look at that!"

"Someone's in love with you, Leanne!"

"Whose writing is it?"

Leanne slowly turned the pages. She was fascinated. I knew the safest place for me was in the middle of the gang. I wiped the sweat off my forehead and marched straight up.

"Let's have an investigation," I said.

The investigation started at break and continued in the dinner hour. We checked the handwriting of every third year boy. We did it alphabetically (my idea), starting with Jamal Ali and ending with Ian Street. That gave me time to quietly remove all my workbooks, essays, membership cards and homework diary. They all went into my bag, and my bag was hidden in the cloakrooms.

Several people thought it was Bashir. Bashir was often seen with Leanne. He wrote in blue biro, like the writing in the book, and the capital Gs were identical.

"Looks like we should call off the investigation," I said.

"It's nothing like my writing!" protested Bash.

"Course it is!" I said. "Look at the loops!"

"You can see it isn't!" said Bash. "Why are you trying to frame me?"

I tried to look innocent.

"Maybe it's *your* writing," said Bash.

Suddenly all the eyes were focused on me. I smiled calmly. "Check it out if you like," I said.

We went to my desk. I searched through it for a book. "Would you believe it?" I said. "They're all at home."

"No," said Bash. "We wouldn't believe it."

"All right," I said. "Give us some paper."

Someone handed me a sheet of paper. I began to write, in a strange, spiky style.

"That ain't your writing!" said Bash.

"Who's writing it then?" I said.

"Why'd you change it, Streetie?" asked Bash.

I was in big trouble now. I had to think fast. "All right," I said. "I'll bring my books in tomorrow, then we'll see who's right!"

I whirled away, straight into Leanne, who had watched the whole thing.

Chapter 5

There was only one choice open to me. I had to rewrite every single thing I'd written. The rough books, the stories, the essays, even the details on my bus pass.

First, I had to buy all the equipment: new books, paper, Tipp-Ex, and various colour pens. That wasn't going to come cheap.

"Can I borrow some money, Mum?" I said.

"What for?" she said.

"Books and pens for school, Mum," I said.

Mum thought I was off my head. "You get them off the school!" she said.

"Not any more, Mum. Government cuts."

Mum said I had to earn the money. That meant cleaning the windows, the car, the front yard and the rabbit.

I bought the gear. I shut myself in my room and set to work. I started on an essay which had taken me all week. This time it took me half an hour. Funny what you can do when you put your mind to it.

The first essay was followed by a second, then a third, then a fourth. They were all written in the strange spiky style I had invented that afternoon.

Then I had to go through them again, putting in the teachers' comments. It was painful having to write "YOU FOOLISH BOY, WHY IS THIS WORK NOT FINISHED?" and "SEE ME" over and over again. It was like punching yourself in the face. No wonder I hated school.

Hours passed, and on I scribbled. The words didn't mean anything any more. They were just like insects, crawling over the pages. After a while they seemed to take on a life of their own. I could see them crawling up the walls and over the floor. I was badly over-tired. But there was no stopping till I'd finished the lot.

I don't know what time it was when my head hit the pillow. My hand was so cramped it felt like a twisted claw. But I had done it.

Next morning I sailed into school, whistling a happy tune. My bag was full to bursting with the books I'd rewritten. I took them straight into class and unloaded them on to the desk.

"There you go," I said. "Check it out."

"What's that?" said Bash, without much interest.

"My writing," I replied.

"No, we're not bothered now," said Bash.

I couldn't believe it. "Why not?" I said.

"We've got the culprit," said Bash.

This, needless to say, was surprising news. "Who's that then?" I said, innocently.

Bash tapped his nose. "You'll have to wait till the chat show," he said.

No one was letting on.

The day of the chat show came, and I still didn't know who they'd found guilty. Even so, I took great care to keep writing in that strange spiky style. It wasn't easy, especially with a hand still aching from that awful night.

At last, it was time for Media Studies. Mrs Walker took us down to the library, and we set up the camera, the table and the chairs, just like before.

"Make way for the master director," I said, and focused the camera. "Clear off, Jamal," I said. "That's Leanne's chair."

"No it isn't," said Jamal.

The others agreed. Jamal was doing the interview.

"Who's being interviewed?" I asked.

"Ssh!" said Bash. "They're not supposed to know!"

"I get you," I said.

Silence fell. The camera rolled. Jamal smiled. "Hello and welcome to the 3S Chat Show," he began. "I'm Jamal Ali and in a moment I am going to interview a special guest."

The other chair was still empty. The suspense grew. I felt a tap on the shoulder.

"Leanne's taking over the camera now," said Bash.

"What?" I said. At that moment I was seized by three of the lads. They frogmarched me to the front, and sat me in the empty chair.

"Ladies and gentlemen," said Jamal. "My first guest – Ian Street."

There was a round of applause and cheers.

"All right," I said nervously.

"Now tell me, Ian," said Jamal. "Do you have much in common?"

My blood froze. "Who with?" I muttered.

Jamal slowly removed a tatty piece of paper from his pocket.

With horror, I recognized the note I'd written a few days before:

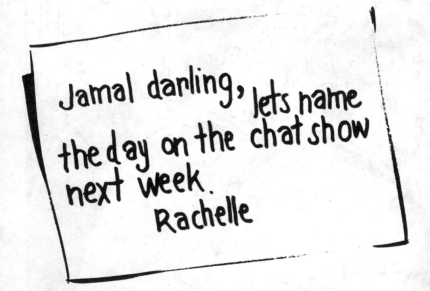

Jamal darling, lets name the day on the chat show next week.
Rachelle

With great drama, Jamal then produced
the dreaded exercise book.

"Leanne Grant. Leanne Grant. Leanne
Grant," it said, in exactly the same writing.

"I think we know who with," said Jamal.